HOW GRIZZLY FOUND GRATITUDE

Written By Dennis Mathew

Illustrated By Taylor Barron

Happy Birthday, Krish!

atmosphere press

Also by Dennis Mathew

Bello the Cello
My WILD First Day of School

Published by Atmosphere Press

atmospherepress.com

This book is dedicated to...

My friend Travis B. for planting the seed to write this book.
My friends in New England who became my home away from home.
My Girls, Sini and Rhema. You will always be "home" to me.

A special thanks to my "inner circle" for reviewing this project
to get it ready for the world to see.
You know who you are. I couldn't have done this without you.

Once upon a time, Grizzly got lost in the wild.
He couldn't find his way home no matter how hard he tried.

He still kept searching but he became sad, lonely, and weary.
One day, when he couldn't take another step, he stopped
to catch his breath.

Seeing the resting Grizzly, Bird stopped by.
"Hey friend! I've never seen you around here.
Are you new to the neighborhood?"
she asked curiously.

"No, Bird, I was looking for food
and wandered far from home.
Now I'm lost," Grizzly admitted in defeat.

"Oh my! How long have you been lost?"
Bird wondered.

"I honestly don't know.
I've lost all track of time,"
Grizzly answered sadly.

"Hey, I know just the thing that will cheer you up!"
Bird said, and flew off in a flurry.

Grizzly didn't know what to expect,
but he followed her anyway.

Bird flew and flew with Grizzly carefully pawing behind her.
And soon, they came upon a bear's favorite treasure.

There hanging from a huge tree, hidden in plain sight, was an
abandoned honeycomb, drenched with Grizzly's favorite:
ooey, gooey, golden honey.

Grizzly stood tall and gleefully threw his face
into the honeycomb, devouring every drop
that he could slurp, sip, drink, and chew.

He was full. Oh, so full.
Grizzly licked his fingertips.
"Yum! That was scrumptious!
It tasted just like the honey back home," he said.

"What was home like?" Bird asked.

"Oh you wouldn't believe it," Grizzly said,
as fond memories of his home flooded his mind.

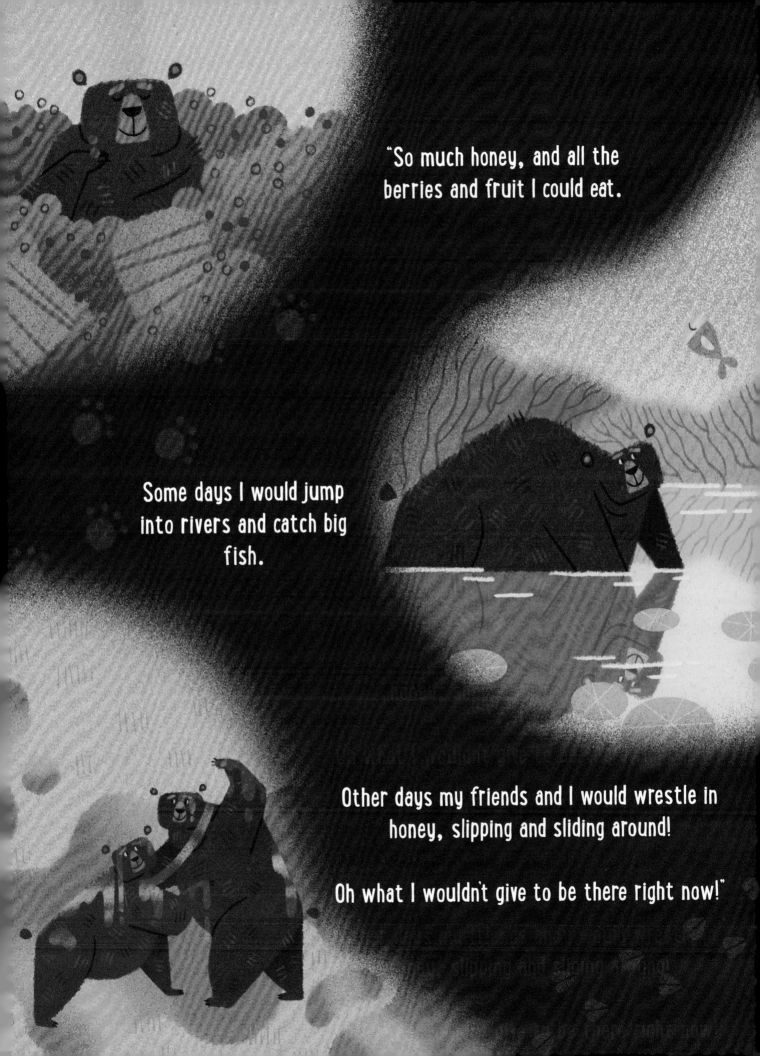

"So much honey, and all the berries and fruit I could eat.

Some days I would jump into rivers and catch big fish.

Other days my friends and I would wrestle in honey, slipping and sliding around!

Oh what I wouldn't give to be there right now!"

Bird comforted Grizzly,
"Well one thing I've learned is,
even when things don't go our
way, if we have gratitude,
we can be happy."

"Gratitude? Does it taste like honey?" Grizzly
questioned.

"No, Grizzly. It's not something you eat."

"Does it fly like you? Does it scratch its back
on a tree like me?"

"No, Grizzly. It's not a living thing like you and me
either! Gratitude means to be thankful,"
Bird enlightened the bear.

It turns out that Bird's friends were not too far away.
They were soon about to meet her burly new friend.

"Well, what do I even have to be thankful for?"
Grizzly did not sound happy.
"I have absolutely lost everything!"
Bird listened to the anger,
the sadness, and the hurt in his voice.

She gently consoled him, "There was a time when I didn't know these woods. I was a young bird without a home as well. But that was before I found my friends."

"The Squirrels helped me find a home.

Wolf and Owl kept watch over me at night.

Beaver and Badger helped me find food."

"Life can be hard sometimes.
But having gratitude can make the
journey easier," Bird said.

Grizzly thought for a moment.
"I guess I can be thankful for the cave I
found while I was wandering lost.
At least I don't have to
search for a place to stay."

"I'm also thankful for honey.
I am sure glad I'm not hungry!
But most importantly,
I am really happy that I am not alone,
that I have someone to talk to
and someone to listen."

Bird could see it.
Grizzly was starting
to have a change of heart.

"Bird, I'm sorry I was rude.
I've been sad for so long that I guess
I just get angry easily
and sometimes I forget to be kind."

"You're forgiven, my friend," Bird kindly replied.
They were watching the sun set in the distance.
"Tomorrow's a new day.
And sometimes, we all need a fresh start."

Bird's gratitude rubbed off on Grizzly.
He became happier the more
he was around Bird and her friends.

Days, weeks, months, and seasons went by.
Grizzly still remembered where he was from,
but he was also getting comfortable
in his new environment.

Together they all started going
on new adventures.

Grizzly taught his friends
to fish,

to play "Honeycomb Toss,"

and "Dodge the Dirt."

Bird's friends showed Grizzly their ways too.
Grizzly tried to eat like the Squirrels,

howl like Wolf,

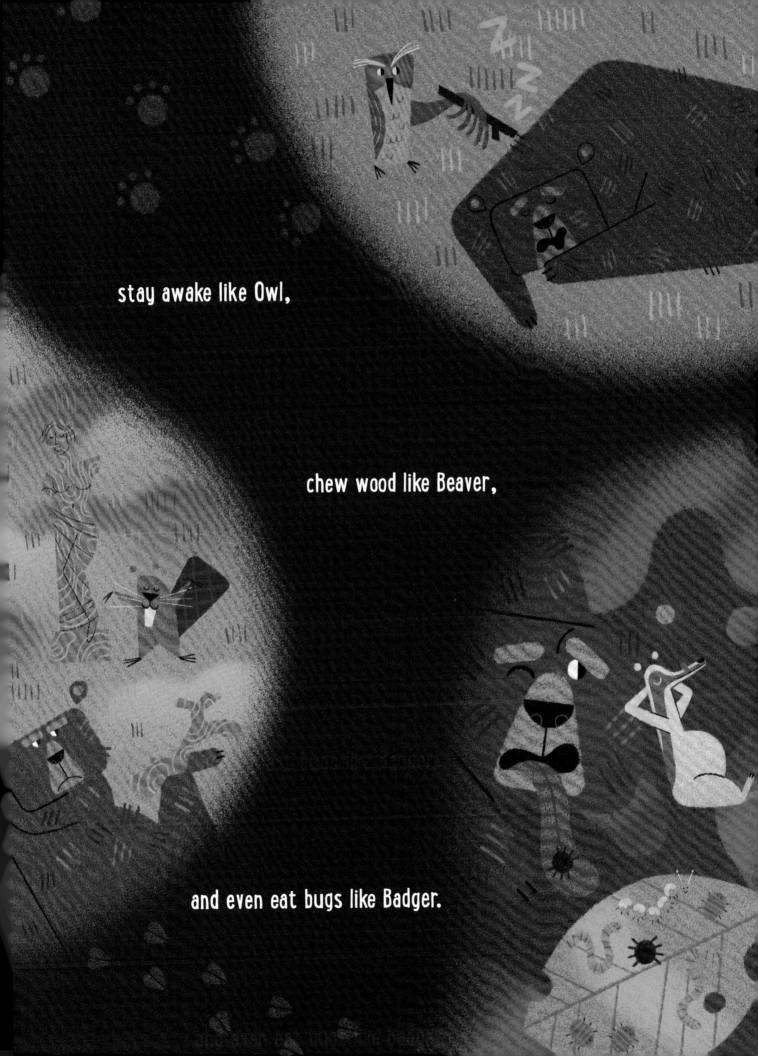

stay awake like Owl,

chew wood like Beaver,

and even eat bugs like Badger.

One day, when they were exploring,
the group felt thirsty.
As they searched for water,
they came up on a roaring river.

While they were quenching their thirst,
Bird saw something in the distance.
She looked closely and was suddenly shocked!
She whispered, "Grizzly!"

Grizzly looked up and couldn't believe his eyes.
Far away, there was a sleuth of grizzlies fishing.

Grizzly didn't know them,
but for the first time in a long time,
he was seeing other grizzlies.
It reminded him of his old home.

Bird even had an idea.
"Maybe they can help you
find your way back home!"

Was Grizzly going to stay or was he going to leave?
his friends wondered.

They were getting ready to leave when one of the
bears spotted Grizzly and his friends.
"Hey! What are you doing over there? Come join us!"
he hollered and walked over to Grizzly.

"Just spending time with family!" Grizzly replied.
The visiting bear looked confused.
"What about you all?" Grizzly inquired.

"Oh just looking for fish! We were
just about to leave."

"Well, come again sometime!
There's lots of honey around here
too," Grizzly added.

"Sounds like a plan,"
the departing grizzly agreed.
"See you next time!"

As the sleuth started leaving,
Bird couldn't believe what happened.

"Why didn't you ask them to help you
find your home?" she asked Grizzly.

With the slightest smile
and gleam in his eye, Grizzly replied,
"This is my home. This is where
I now belong: with all of you."

Grizzly's friends gathered
around him in a sweet embrace.
The once-lost grizzly now had a family.

"Home is not just a place," Grizzly added.
"Home is also who you are with."

In the end, Grizzly found gratitude,
and it was gratitude that helped
Grizzly find a new home.

About Atmosphere Press

Atmosphere Press is an independent, full-service publisher for excellent books in all genres and for all audiences. Learn more about what we do at atmospherepress.com.

We encourage you to check out some of Atmosphere's latest children's book releases, which are available online and via order from your local bookstore:

Beau Wants to Know, a picture book by Brian Sullivan

The King's Drapes, a picture book by Jocelyn Tambascio

You are the Moon, a picture book by Shana Rachel Diot

Onionhead, a picture book by Gary Ziskovsky

Odo and the Stranger, a picture book by Mark Johnson

Jack and the Lean Stalk, a picture book by Raven Howell

Brave Little Donkey, a picture book by Rachel L. Pieper

Buried Treasure: A Cool Kids Adventure, by Anne Krebbs

The Magpie and The Turtle, a picture book by Timothy Yeahquo

The Alligator Wrestler: A Girls Can Do Anything Book, by Carmen Petro

The Sky Belongs to the Dreamers, a picture book by J.P. Hostetler

I Will Love You Forever and Always, by Sarah Thomas Mariano

Oscar the Loveable Seagull, a picture book by Mark Johnson

Makani and the Tiki Mikis, a picture book by Kosta Gregory

Sola Gratia.
Sola Fide.

About the Author

Dennis Mathew is a husband, father, elementary school speech pathologist, songwriter and author. For over 20 years Dennis has had the joy and honor of working with children in public schools and churches. In 2017, he launched his authorship, bringing children's stories integrating social emotional wholeness, language enrichment, critical thinking, conflict resolution and character development to life. His first book, "Bello the Cello", an award winning short story for children, since being released in December of 2018, as of the beginning of 2021, has sold over 10,000 copies. His second book, "My Wild First Day of School", brings humor, rhythm and rhyme into encouraging students to seize the moment and take charge of their first day. To date, Dennis Mathew has had the privilege of reaching over 70,000 students with his books and originally written songs, both in person and virtually, in the United States, Mexico, the UK, the United Arab Emirates and Africa.

About the Illustrator

Taylor Barron is an artist and illustrator from Seattle, Washington living in Paris, France. She graduated with a Bachelor's of Fine Art in Digital Art and Animation from DigiPen Institute of Technology in 2017. After working in animation for a few years, she decided to become an independent artist and began to work on children's books. Since that time she has illustrated several children's books and will continue to work with authors around the globe, bringing their stories to life. She is inspired by traveling, music, animation, and fashion, and loves to use lots of color in her work!

BooksByDennis.com
Instagram: @booksbydennis
Twitter: @storiesbydennis
dennismmathew@gmail.com
BooksByDennis.Bandcamp.com